KU-541-635

This Walker book belongs to:

For Stephanie Lamb
and Rosebank Primary School, Leeds

First published 1998 by Walker Books Ltd
87 Vauxhall Walk, London SE11 5HJ

This edition published 2021

2 4 6 8 10 9 7 5 3 1

© 1998 Nick Sharratt

The right of Nick Sharratt to be identified as author/illustrator of this work has been asserted by him
in accordance with the Copyright, Designs and Patents Act 1988

This book has been typeset in Highlander

Printed in China

All rights reserved. No part of this book may be reproduced, transmitted or stored in an information retrieval system
in any form or by any means, graphic, electronic or mechanical, including photocopying, taping and recording,
without prior written permission from the publisher.

British Library Cataloguing in Publication Data:
a catalogue record for this book is available from the British Library

ISBN 978-1-5295-0456-9

www.walker.co.uk

Dinosaurs' Day Out

Nick Sharratt

WALKER BOOKS

AND SUBSIDIARIES

LONDON • BOSTON • SYDNEY • AUCKLAND

Meet Dexter and Daisy. Today they're going on a car journey to visit their friend Delilah.

Delilah lives a long way away so they need to look at a map to see how to get there.

"This is the town where we live," says Dexter.

GREAT BIGSVILLE

LITTLEBURY

BIGSVILLE ROAD

RUSHALONG ROAD

ZOOMAWAY AIRPORT

WHIZZPAST WAY

MIDDLESWICK

KEY

main road

road

river

railway

town

lake

forest

airport

port

petrol station

railway station

windmill

castle

0 1 2 3 4 5 miles

0 1 2 3 4 5 kilometres

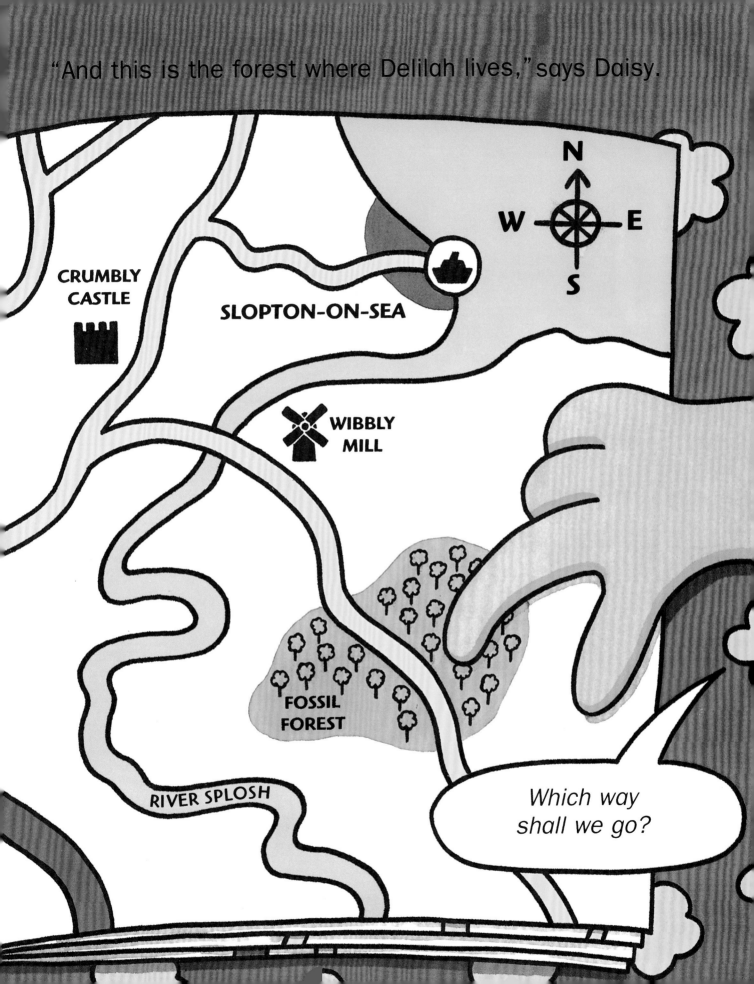

Daisy gets her backpack and Dexter checks
the weather forecast.
"Great! It's sunny where we're going,"
he calls to Daisy.

They try to make sure they've got everything. Can you help them? What can you see that they might need to take with them on their journey? Do you remember seeing the car keys?

And where did they leave Delilah's present?

Off they go, along the road,
past the school, down the hill
and into town.

They drive right through the town and past the railway station. "Should we turn left and go towards the airport?" asks Daisy.

"Whoops!" says Dexter. "We've forgotten the map!" Which way do *you* think they should go?

They drive past the lake.
"Eek!" cries Daisy suddenly.
"The red light's flashing ...

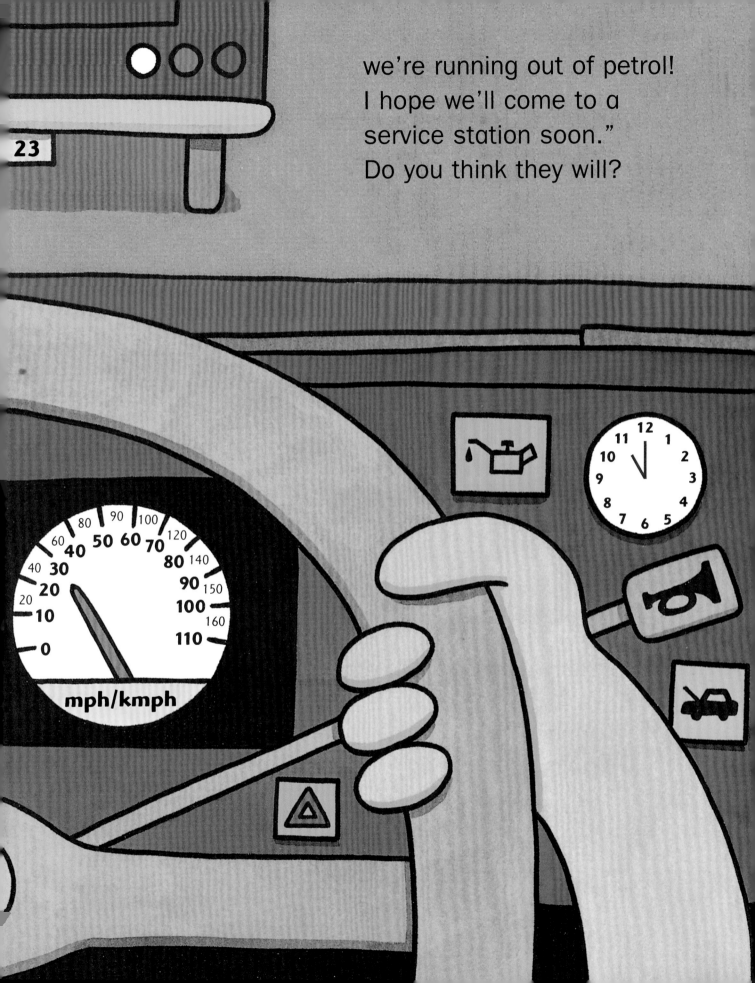

we're running out of petrol!
I hope we'll come to a
service station soon."
Do you think they will?

23

Luckily it's not long before they can stop and buy some petrol. Dexter's feeling hungry so they go to the café.

Daisy fancies some toast and hot chocolate. But Dexter just can't decide what to eat! Can you choose something for him from the menu?

After their break they turn off the Whizzpast Way
and drive along a country road until
they come to a junction.
"Which way now?" asks Daisy.
"I wish we'd brought the map!"
says Dexter.
Can you help them?

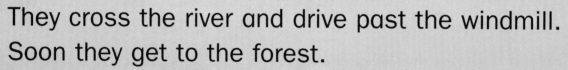

They cross the river and drive past the windmill.
Soon they get to the forest.
"I think Delilah must live somewhere near here,"
says Daisy. "Let's drive up this hill to get a
better look."

It's not a hill.
It's their friend Delilah!